TREEMONISHA

ANGELA SHELF MEDEARIS

FROM THE OPERA BY

SCOTT JOPLIN

ILLUSTRATED BY

MICHAEL BRYANT

Henry Holt and Company
New York

Dedicated to Adrienne Betz and Marc Aronson,
my friends and editors, and in memory of Vera Brodsky Lawrence,
who preserved Scott Joplin's work for the enjoyment of everyone.
—A. S. M.

To Walter, Un OK, and Donald
—M. B.

Henry Holt and Company, Inc.
Publishers since 1866
115 West 18th Street
New York, New York 10011

Henry Holt is a registered
trademark of Henry Holt and Company, Inc.

Text copyright © 1995 by Angela Shelf Medearis
Illustrations copyright © 1995 by Michael Bryant
All rights reserved.
Published in Canada by Fitzhenry & Whiteside Ltd.,
195 Allstate Parkway, Markham, Ontario L3R 4T8.

Library of Congress Cataloging-in-Publication Data
Medearis, Angela Shelf, date.
Treemonisha / by Angela Shelf Medearis; illustrated by Michael Bryant.
Summary: Treemonisha, the daughter of freed slaves in the post–Civil War South,
gets an education and devotes herself to lifting her people
out of poverty and ignorance. Based on an opera by Scott Joplin.
1. Afro-Americans—History—1863–1877—Juvenile fiction.
[1. Afro-Americans—History—1863–1877—Fiction.]   I. Bryant, Michael, ill.
II. Joplin, Scott, 1868–1917. Treemonisha.   III. Title.
PZ7.M51274Tr   1995   [Fic]—dc20   94-48933

ISBN 0-8050-1748-8

First Edition—1995
Printed in the United States of America
on acid-free paper. ∞
1 3 5 7 9 10 8 6 4 2

The artist used watercolor and colored pencil
on Arches paper to create the illustrations for this book.

AUTHOR'S NOTE

I first saw *Treemonisha* performed on a videotape of the Houston Grand Opera production. Thrilled by the wonderful music and the history of Joplin's struggle to bring his work to the stage, I set out to translate the spirit of the opera into a picture book. Of course, moving from stage to page I had to make some changes. Though I followed his plot, and divided the story into acts, this book is not meant to re-create the entire opera as it appears on stage. But when Joplin's words were particularly lively or important, I used excerpts from his original libretto. In particular, "The Special Tree," "The Ring Dance," and a few of Zodzetrick's rhymes are adaptations of Joplin's text. I hope that if you enjoy the book you have the chance to see the opera that inspired it.

OVERTURE

CHILD, LONG BEFORE you were even thought about, two old folks named Ned and Monisha lived on a small plot of land, deep in the piney woods of Arkansas. The joy of their lives was their pretty daughter, Treemonisha.

Treemonisha was born in 1866, shortly after freedom came. Now, that was a jubilee time! Lots of folks left the plantation and moved up North. But Ned, Monisha, and a few of their friends decided to work together, buy some land, and call their homestead Liberty. Day after day everyone worked hard building new cabins, plowing their fields, and planting seeds in the rich black dirt.

All the folks in Liberty dreamed of a better life for themselves and their children. But Ned and Monisha seemed to have the biggest dreams of all. They wanted Treemonisha to go to school. Before slavery was abolished, it was against the law to teach a black person to read or write. Now that they were free, the people of Liberty wanted to be educated.

Ned often did odd jobs for a white woman in a nearby town. As payment, she agreed to teach his daughter. Soon, Treemonisha was the only black person for miles around who could read, write, and do her numbers. Every night, Ned and Monisha sat side by side, smiling proudly as their daughter read aloud.

Ned and Monisha saved their money for years so that Treemonisha could go away to school. The good people of Liberty also gave whatever they could to help her. Treemonisha hoped that once she was educated, she could repay them by teaching their children. Cheers rang out when she boarded the train to go away to school. Everyone's hopes for a better life rode off with her.

While Treemonisha was away, an evil little man named Zodzetrick began causing trouble in Liberty.

Everywhere Zodzetrick went he seemed to plant seeds of bitterness. He'd sprinkle a touch of jealousy, spite, envy, and hate into his conversations. Then he'd water his words with a little superstition, evil eyes, fixes, and the like. The dreadful mixture of fear and malice spread out over anyone who listened to him. He frightened the people with horrible stories of misfortune, ill winds, ghosts, and goblins.

"Give me your money, or no matter what you say or do, everywhere you go, evil will follow you," threatened Zodzetrick.

For years, Zodzetrick kept most of the people in Liberty in fear and poverty. He made many of them believe that he could tell the future and cast spells. Some foolish folks would use their last bit of money to buy his useless potions and conjures. Then that old trickster would sit back and laugh as he filled up his money bag.

Zodzetrick called himself the King of Goofer Dust Land, which was in the darkest part of the piney woods. He lived there with his assistant, Luddud, and all the outcasts and misfits from Liberty. Every night, they held conjure meetings at their camp, which was hidden deep in the forest.

— ACT ONE —

ONE COOL EVENING, a few days after Treemonisha had graduated from college and returned home, Zodzetrick appeared. He watched from behind some bushes as the tall young woman and her friend Remus read aloud. Then he spied on Ned and Monisha, who were working in their garden. Zodzetrick laughed to himself as he opened the garden gate. He danced a funny little dance down the rows of mustard greens and snap beans. Then he stopped suddenly in front of Monisha.

"If you buy my bag of luck, it will cheer you when you're sad." Zodzetrick slowly swung the bag back and forth, back and forth, back and forth. "Just one bag will ward off everything that's bad."

"Will it really bring us good luck and happiness?" asked Monisha as she eagerly reached for the bag.

"Dear lady," answered Zodzetrick, smiling slyly as he swung it just out of her reach. "Listen closely to everything I say. If you buy this bag of luck, good fortune will come to you each day!"

He snapped his fingers and the bag disappeared into the folds of his cloak. "Just place eight coins in the palm of my hand and soon you'll be the happiest woman in the land." Zodzetrick bowed and held out his hand.

"Don't be silly, Monisha," Ned burst out as he pushed Zodzetrick away. "You can't buy luck! He only wants our money."

"Ah, foolish man," taunted Zodzetrick as he swirled his colorful cloak around him. The bag reappeared in his hand, seeming to glow in the evening light. "I must tell you plain and bold, this little bag of luck is worth its weight in gold!" Ned shook his head and went back to his work.

Zodzetrick skipped down the narrow path and leaned close to Ned. "You just better be careful and watch what you say and do, because I'm the Goofer Dust Man, King of Goofer Dust Land, and strange things happen when I say 'Hee Hoo.' " He wiggled his short, stubby fingers in Ned's face. "Yes, strange things happen when I say 'Hee Hoo.' "

"Sir," said Treemonisha as she approached Zodzetrick. "My father told me all about you and your phony potions. Why are you cheating your own people? Don't you know when you hurt your own race, you're hurting yourself, too? Most of the folks in Liberty are poor because of you. They fear you because all you ever talk about is evil. Then they spend all their money buying your bags of luck. I'm not going to stand for any more of it."

"Little lady, don't you dare try to tangle with me! I've got far more power than you can see." Zodzetrick clapped his hands, hopped on one foot and then the other. "Yes, I sell these bags of luck, 'tis true. But take care, gal, I just might send bad luck to you!"

"Be quiet, man," said Remus as he stepped between Zodzetrick and Treemonisha. "You can't fool Treemonisha. She has a level head and a good education. She's teaching me, too! I

10

know that there's no such thing as a bag of luck!" Remus put his arm around Treemonisha. "What's more, we're going to stop all your foolishness in this neighborhood. From now on, things are going to be different around here!"

Zodzetrick stepped back from Remus, hunched his shoulders, and made an X in the dust. He turned around and around in the center of the X, east, west, north, and south. He clapped his hands loudly, four times. Then the King of Goofer Dust Land opened up his conjure bag, took out a pinch of black powder, and blew it toward Treemonisha and Remus.

"Hee Hoo, Hee Hoo. Now I've fixed both of you." Zodzetrick dusted off his hands and adjusted his top hat. "I don't care what y'all say. I'll never, never, ever change my ways. I'm going now, but I'll be back soon, long before another full moon."

Treemonisha shook her finger at Zodzetrick. "I don't believe in any of your nonsense. I'm going to tell everyone I know that there's no such thing as buying luck. I'm going to start a school here and educate my people. We're going to work together to make Liberty a good place to live, in spite of you."

Zodzetrick stuck out his chin and stretched his skinny neck out like a turtle. "How dare you interfere!" He glared at Treemonisha. "We'll see who has the stronger power around here!"

"Get away from her, man," Remus replied angrily. "We've had enough of your foolishness." He picked Zodzetrick up by the collar as if he were a puppy dog and shook him until his shirt buttons popped open and his socks fell down. Then he set him on the ground outside the garden gate.

Zodzetrick seemed to swell up like a toad. "Mark my words, if it's the last thing I ever do, I'll get even with all of you!" And with that, Zodzetrick spun around and around until he melted into a blur of rainbow colors. Then he ran off into the woods.

FALL DRIFTED onto the plantation along with the beautiful yellow, orange, and red leaves on the trees. The crops had all been gathered. A brisk wind whistled through the newly harvested fields, filling the air with autumn sounds.

All the neighbors were coming to help Ned shuck the small mountain of corn he had gathered in the barnyard. Monisha and her daughter had been cleaning and baking since before the sun came up. Treemonisha was excited because after the work was finished, there would be a dance. While she dusted, Treemonisha practiced the steps to the newest dance, the Slow Drag. Then she Cakewalked around the kitchen using her broom as a partner. Holding her head high and kicking her legs out stiffly, Treemonisha smiled at the thought of dancing with Remus that night. "My, my," Treemonisha whispered to the broom as she dropped into a curtsey. "You dance divinely." She stood up and quickly began sweeping again when Monisha appeared in the room.

Late that afternoon the cornhuskers arrived, some in mule-drawn wagons and others on horseback. Everyone milled around the yard, laughing and greeting neighbors they hadn't seen for weeks.

"Here comes Parson Alltalk to say the blessing over the harvest!" someone shouted. Parson Alltalk stopped his wagon and waved to the crowd.

"Looks like these folks are all ready to work, so let me commence my blessing." Parson Alltalk climbed up on the back of the wagon. The cornhuskers eagerly gathered in a circle. "I just want to say a few words of good advice from the Good Book to you fine folks before you start working," he began.

"Say on, Parson!" shouted Ned.

Parson Alltalk hooked his thumbs in his lapels, rocked back and forth on his heels, and began his sermon. "Listen here, friends," he said, holding his hands out wide and smiling at the crowd, "love one another! That's just plain good advice."

"That's right!" Monisha whooped.

"Live like brothers and sisters. Now, remember all I say to you. Because it's just plain good advice!"

"It sure is!" hollered one man.

"Good advice, Parson, good advice!" roared another as the crowd began swaying.

"Listen here, friends," the Parson pleaded. "Don't tell lies and steal, it just ain't right. Now, remember all I say to you. Because it's just plain good advice!"

"Preach on, brother!" Remus said, tapping his foot in time to the Parson's rhythmic speech. The crowd clapped their hands and shouted in response to the Parson's words.

"Love your neighbor!"

"Uh-huh!"

"Don't do your neighbor no harm!"

"Well!"

"Always live like brothers and sisters."

"That's right!"

"Don't tell lies and steal."

"Say that, Parson, say that!"

"Speak the truth!"

"Oh, yes!"

"Now, remember all I say to you," Parson Alltalk shouted, "because it's just plain good advice!"

"Yes, yes!" screamed Monisha as she waved her arms in the air. Ned fanned her with his hat. Parson Alltalk wiped the sweat from his forehead and leaned closer to the crowd.

"Now, does you feel like you been redeemed?"

"Yes, indeed we do, Parson," the crowd hollered joyfully.

"I say, does you feel like you been redeemed?" Parson Alltalk clapped his hands.

"Oh, yes," the crowd roared back, "we feel like we've been redeemed."

"Well, say Amen, somebody." Parson Alltalk smiled down at the crowd.

"Amen!" cried the crowd. "Oh, yes! Amen!"

"Amen, amen, and amen. Bless you! Bless all of you and this bountiful harvest, too. Now you may commence working." Parson Alltalk wiped his face with his handkerchief and put his hat back on. Then he shook hands with Ned and the rest of the men. Everyone waved good-bye as the Parson traveled over the hill and out of sight.

-ACT TWO-

TREEMONISHA saw her friend Lucy among the crowd of laughing workers who filled the yard. She looked especially fine. "That's a beautiful wreath you're wearing," Treemonisha said. The bright fall leaves and flowers Lucy wore made her look like an African queen.

"Thank you," answered Lucy with a smile. "I can make one for you, too! We can use some of the lovely leaves on this tree. Then we'll decorate it with flowers."

Monisha overheard Lucy and called to them from the window. "Girls, don't take any leaves from that tree."

"Oh, Mother, what's so special about this tree? These leaves are the prettiest around."

Monisha hesitated and then said, "Treemonisha, come inside for a moment, please." Puzzled, the young woman went inside the cabin and sat down.

Monisha wiped her hands on her apron and settled into her rocking chair. The old chair creaked sorrowfully. Monisha took both of her daughter's hands into her own.

"Treemonisha," she said. "I want to tell you a story about that tree. This is hard for me to tell you, so let me sing it as a song:

The Story of the Special Tree

One autumn night in bed I was laying
Just eighteen years ago,
I heard a dear little baby crying
while loudly Ned did snore,
And the baby's crying seemed to be
somewhere near that special tree.
I called to Ned and said, 'Wake up,
A baby is crying outside the door.'
But Ned said, 'You're only dreaming, my dear,'
and went to sleep once more.
It was twelve o'clock, or just before,
when the rain fell hard and fast,
the baby's cries I heard no more
and I went to sleep at last.
The next morning at ten o'clock
the hot sun was shining down
and I went out into the yard to see
what that crying sound could be.
And there in rags a baby lay
sheltered by that tree's cool shade,
I took that child into our home
and now that darling girl is grown.
All I've said to you is true
and, Treemonisha, that baby girl was you."

Treemonisha began to cry. "I don't know what to think. What happened to my real parents?" Monisha put her arms around her daughter.

"We've never been able to find them. But I'm sure your parents loved you, dear. Maybe they just couldn't do any better. All I know is that you've been a great blessing to your papa and me."

Monisha thought back over the years and smiled. "When you were small, you were happiest when playing underneath that tree. I named you Monisha first, but then I changed your name to Treemonisha, because that tree is a special part of you. If it hadn't been for the sheltering leaves on that tree, the cold rain or the hot sun would have sent you to your grave."

Treemonisha wiped away her tears and looked into her mother's eyes. "I'm sorry I didn't tell you sooner, baby," Monisha whispered. "I just couldn't. I didn't know how."

Treemonisha took a deep breath and answered, "I know you both love me. I just need some time to think about all this."

"I understand," said Monisha softly.

"Lucy and I will go into the woods and find another tree. We'll be back soon." She kissed her mother good-bye and went outside to find her friend.

Treemonisha stopped when she came to the special tree. She put her arms around its majestic old trunk. Then she laid her head against the rough bark and started to cry.

"I wish you could talk."

The wind blew gently through the leaves. Treemonisha wiped her face and gently patted the tree trunk. Then she called to Lucy, and the two young women ran into the woods.

AFTER THE BLESSING, Ned divided the cornhuskers into two teams. Andy was chosen as leader of one team, Remus the other. Two huge piles of corn were stacked in the barnyard. Everyone raced to see who could shuck their pile of corn first. After all the corn was finished, there would be feasting and dancing until midnight.

Soon, the last ear had been shucked and thrown into the baskets. Mounds of corn lay bare and gleaming like yellow gold in the waning sunlight. Ned held up Andy's hand and declared his team the winners of the corn-shucking race.

"Well, Remus," Andy said, "looks like every year I gets a little faster and you gets a little slower."

"I'd pat you on the back," Remus said, "but you're doing such a good job of congratulating yourself, both of your hands are in my way."

"I hope you can call the dances faster than you can shuck corn," Andy teased as he took his fiddle out of its battered case.

"Don't matter about how fast I call 'em," Remus replied, "long as I holler loud. That's the only way I can cover up your bad fiddle-playing." Andy threw an ear of corn at Remus. Remus caught it and pretended to play it like a fiddle.

The barnyard was filled with laughter and cheering. All the hard work was finally done. Now it was time to dance! Andy tuned his fiddle as the others moved the baskets of corn out of the way. The men laid wooden planks across the barnyard. The dancers hurriedly formed a circle. Andy swung into a fast tune and Remus sang out:

"There was a man before the war
Oh, we're going around.
Who didn't like his mother-in-law
Oh, we're going around.
I know we'll have a jolly good time
Oh, we're going around
Because the weather's very fine
Oh, we're going around.
Girls all smiling, goin' round
Girls all smiling, goin' round
Smiling sweetly, goin' round
Keep on goin' around.

Oh, boys all smiling, goin' round
Boys all smiling, goin' round
Smiling sweetly, goin' round
Keep on goin' around.
Let your steps be light and neat.
Oh, keep goin' around,
Be careful how you shake your feet,
Oh, keep goin' around.
Keep going around, keep going around,
swing and swing and keep goin' around!"

Bare feet slapped the wooden planks in time to the music. Hands clapped and fingers snapped. Laughter rang out as couples met, swung around and around, then sashayed down the line. The men gallantly bowed to their partners. The ladies elegantly fanned out their neatly patched calico skirts as they sank into deep curtseys. Then the couples linked arms and swung around again.

The fading light softened the dancers' coarse clothing. Faces lined with hard work and worry were made beautiful by laughter.

When the song ended, the dancers clapped and clapped. Andy and Remus smiled and bowed to the left and to the right. Then Andy started up another merry tune.

Monisha was busy serving punch and cake to their guests. When she finally had a moment to rest, she looked among the dancers for her daughter and Lucy.

"Have you seen Treemonisha or Lucy?" she asked her husband.

"No, I haven't seen either one of them for quite a while," Ned answered as he looked around the crowded barnyard.

Monisha twisted the ends of her apron together nervously. "They've been gone a long time. Maybe someone ought to go look for them."

Just then, Lucy stumbled into the circle of dancers and collapsed. Her mouth was covered with a handkerchief and her hands were tied behind her. The dancers gathered around her.

"Move back," Ned said as he quickly untied Lucy. "Give her some air. What happened to you, Lucy?" Ned gently wiped her face with his handkerchief. "Where is Treemonisha?"

"Treemonisha and I went into the woods to pick leaves," Lucy gasped. "We met Zodzetrick and Luddud on the pathway." Lucy leaned heavily on Ned's arm. "They grabbed us and tied us up. I escaped while they were putting Treemonisha on a horse."

Monisha hid her face in her apron and began to cry.

"Don't worry," Remus assured the old couple. "I'll bring Treemonisha back."

Andy pushed his way through the crowd. "I'll go with you, Remus. We'll punish that Zodzetrick and Luddud, too!" The other men gathered around Remus and Andy.

As the men were rushing away, Remus suddenly stopped. He stepped inside the barn and looked around until he found the things he needed. Then he ran after the others into the woods to search for Treemonisha.

— ACT THREE —

AS THE SUN SET and the light melted into darkness, Zodzetrick, Luddud, and Treemonisha traveled deeper and deeper into the piney woods.

It was easy to tell when they were near Goofer Dust Land. Even during the hottest part of the day, the sun refused to shine its warming light into this part of the forest. Trees rose up from massive trunks into a tangle of oddly twisted limbs covered with droopy, gray moss. Somber shadows made the trunks and branches look like hulking monsters. A cold, dank mist swirled around the travelers like steam from a witch's cauldron. Thick vines coiled their tentaclelike stems around Treemonisha as if to drag her even deeper into the cold, wet darkness. Even the horse's hoofs striking the brittle ground sounded like the beat of a death march.

As night fell, a sliver of moon appeared high in the inky sky. Dark clouds swirled around it like a shroud. Skeletal beams of moonlight poked their bony fingers through the trees. The cold, damp air smelled of rotting leaves and vibrated with a bizarre humming sound.

"Hee Hoo, Hee Hoo!" shouted Zodzetrick as he entered the clearing where the conjurers camped.

"Hee Hoo, Hee Hoo," someone answered back. Then one by one Zodzetrick's followers emerged from their weary-looking shacks and huts. They were an odd group of men and women, all outcasts from the neighborhood. Each one wore long necklaces of bones carved into strange figures. Zodzetrick's bags of luck dangled from their waists.

Zodzetrick hopped up on a stump near a small fire. His long, black shadow danced along with him in the firelight. He bounced on one foot and then the other, whirled around twice, and threw a handful of goofer dust into the flames. The fire flared up and an evil-smelling black smoke swirled around his followers. The men and women gathered around their king to hear what he had to say.

"Evil is all about," he whispered, looking around suspiciously. His followers huddled close together. Some of them peered into the shadowy woods.

"There are those here who are in doubt. But I'm the King of Goofer Dust Land. And I will defeat the evil that's at hand." Zodzetrick took a stick and drew a large circle around the fire. Then he jumped back on the stump.

"Behold, the magic circle. All who believe may step in. Those who doubt must stay out. Let the ceremony begin!" Zodzetrick shouted. Luddud began beating the conjurer drum. The conjurer believers stepped inside the circle. In a husky voice, Zodzetrick said:

> "If along the road you're going,
> And all to your true knowing,
> A black cat crosses your path.
> Your bad luck long will last!"

" 'Tis true, 'tis true." The conjurer believers swayed from side to side, shouted, and clapped their hands. "We all believe 'tis true." Luddud beat the drum harder and Zodzetrick chanted faster.

> "If at night while passing a graveyard,
> You shake with fear the most,
> Just step a little faster,
> Before you see a ghost."

" 'Tis true, 'tis true," the conjurer believers roared back. "We all believe 'tis true." Zodzetrick's husky voice rose and fell, as if he were a magician casting a spell.

> "If you're eating food with ease
> And drawing pleasant breath,
> Be careful that you do not sneeze
> Because it's a sign of death!"

27

" 'Tis true, 'tis true," wailed the men and women as they began reeling around the fire. Zodzetrick laughed and threw another handful of goofer dust on the flames. The fire snapped and crackled and licked out at the whirling dancers.

Luddud beat the drum faster and faster. The conjurer believers whipped around as if carried by a strong night wind. The bone necklaces they wore made a weird, tinkling sound. Their open mouths and twisted faces looked monstrous in the light of the flames. Some spun around and around until they fainted and fell on the ground.

Suddenly, Zodzetrick raised both his hands. The drums and the dancing stopped. Everyone was silent.

Zodzetrick quickly jumped off the stump and dragged Treemonisha off her horse and pulled her in front of the crowd. "Now listen to this! This gal is the evil in our midst."

He pointed to the frightened young woman and shouted, "This gal here don't believe in conjury! She's been turning all the people against me!"

"That's the truth," said Luddud. "She's been telling the people not to buy our bags of luck. How are we going to buy our food if we can't sell our bags of luck? This gal must be punished!"

The crowd whispered angrily among themselves. "Punish her!" cried out one of the women. "Punish her! Punish her!" everyone yelled.

"As King of Goofer Dust Land," said Zodzetrick, "I decree that Treemonisha shall die for interfering with me!" Then he grabbed Treemonisha by the arms and dragged her into the woods. His followers rushed along after them. Her screams echoed through the trees.

Treemonisha struggled with all her might when she saw where they had taken her. Nearby, a huge wasps' nest hung from an enormous tree. Thousands of wasps clung to its side, their wings glistening in the moonlight. The loud humming sound they made as they flew in and out of the nest vibrated in Treemonisha's ears.

"Now everyone listen," Zodzetrick whispered. "My plan is best. When I count to three you must shove this gal into that wasps' nest!" Treemonisha tried to get away, but Luddud and the others held her firmly. "One . . . two . . ." said Zodzetrick.

"What's that?" exclaimed Luddud as a strange creature crashed through some bushes near the group. The moonlight and shadows made it seem huge. "A monster!" cried one of the women as it lumbered closer to the crowd.

Luddud let go of Treemonisha and the conjurers ran for their lives. The monster drew closer, and closer, and closer. Treemonisha struggled to free herself, but it was no use. The monster reached out for her.

29

"Treemonisha," whispered Remus as he untied the ropes around her wrists and ankles. "Don't be afraid. It's me, Remus."

"Oh, Remus," cried Treemonisha as she hugged him, "they were going to push me into that wasps' nest! But you came just in time to save me."

Remus looked fearfully at the huge nest and the giant wasps. Then he took Treemonisha's hand and the young couple slipped silently into the woods and hurried home.

"MAMA, PAPA!" shouted Treemonisha. "I'm home!" The old couple hurriedly opened the door and hugged their daughter. "Remus rescued me," Treemonisha said proudly as she smiled at the young man. "He scared the conjurers away with the clothes he took from that old scarecrow in the barn."

Ned laughed and patted Remus on the back. Monisha tearfully shook his hand. "Thank you for saving our child," she said.

Remus smiled shyly. "I'd do anything for Treemonisha."

"Look!" Ned said. "There's a crowd of folks coming this way."

Monisha looked out of the window. "My gracious! Andy and the others have captured Zodzetrick and Luddud!"

Andy shoved Zodzetrick and Luddud through the gate and into the yard. Zodzetrick had lost his colorful cape. His fine clothes were torn, and his elegant top hat had a dent in it. Both men were tied up tightly.

Andy glared at the guilty-looking men. "We went into the conjurers' camp and captured these two rascals!"

"They need a good beating!" shouted one man. "Kick them!" said another. The crowd swirled around Zodzetrick and Luddud angrily. The men began kicking the conjurers. Some of the women hit them with their fists. The two men covered their heads with their arms and crouched in fear. Remus quickly waded into the crowd and stood in front of Zodzetrick and Luddud.

"This isn't the right thing to do," he told the crowd. "Wrong is never right. You shouldn't treat your neighbors this way."

"They're not our neighbors," Andy said angrily.

"We're all neighbors," Remus replied.

"You're just doing evil for evil by hitting them," Treemonisha added. "You're no better than they are. Let's think this through first. There must be a better way."

"Thank you, kind lady," said Zodzetrick with an oily smile.

"Thank you," said Luddud. "Tha—"

"Be quiet," demanded Andy. "You've no right to speak!"

"Please, Andy," pleaded Treemonisha.

Andy looked at Treemonisha. Then he shook his fist at the conjurers. "We ought to punish them somehow. Just think of all the evil they've done! Look at their guilty grins." Zodzetrick and Luddud stopped smiling and tried to look pitiful.

Remus put his hand on Andy's shoulder. "Please, Andy, never do wrong for revenge. Wrong is never right. Please forgive these men for Treemonisha's sake."

"You're nothing but two low-down conjurers," said Andy to Zodzetrick and Luddud. "But I forgive you." Then he untied their hands.

Treemonisha shook hands with Zodzetrick and Luddud. "I've forgiven both of you. Now, no more of your rhymes or your tricks."

Zodzetrick bowed deeply. "Thank you again, madam. We're sorry. Aren't we, Luddud?" Luddud quickly nodded his head.

Treemonisha smiled. "You both are free to go." Zodzetrick and Luddud exchanged surprised glances. Then they swiftly turned to leave.

"Under one condition." The two men stopped and looked at Treemonisha uncertainly. "Zodzetrick, you and your followers are no longer welcome in our town. All of you must leave and never come back. And I want you to return all the money you've taken from our people with your phony bags of luck."

Zodzetrick and Luddud started to protest, but one look from Andy silenced them.

"We'll use the money to build a school here," Treemonisha announced to the crowd. She turned to Zodzetrick and smiled. "I told you I was going to fight against everything you stand for and I meant it. From now on, we're going to work together here in Liberty. We're never going to be slaves to anyone or anything again. Since you all won't work with us, you will have to leave." Treemonisha held out her hand for the money bag.

Grumbling softly, Zodzetrick untied the bag and gave it to her. Then the two conjurers hurried down the road as quickly as they could go. Soon, Zodzetrick and Luddud disappeared over the hill and were never seen in Liberty again.

"Three cheers for Treemonisha!" shouted Andy. Everyone cheered happily.

Treemonisha held the money bag up high. "This is wonderful, but it's not enough. We need to have a leader in our neighborhood. Someone who can advise us wisely and teach us the things we need to know. We need good leadership if we're going to succeed."

Ned nodded his head in agreement. "We've lived in ignorance and fear for much too long."

"You're wise and gentle, Treemonisha," said Andy. "We all need to learn the things you've been taught in school."

"Yes, yes!" shouted the crowd. "Treemonisha should lead us!"

"There are many subjects I can teach," Treemonisha said, "but who will help me?"

Remus linked his arm through hers. "I'll help you, Treemonisha." The young couple smiled at each other.

The evil power that Zodzetrick held over the people was broken at last! With Treemonisha and Remus leading the way, the people of Liberty marched forward, onward into a bright new day.

AFTERWORD

TREEMONISHA is, in a sense, Scott Joplin's musical autobiography. The belief that education is the way to uplift the black race, and the strong feelings of racial pride and unity that are the basis of *Treemonisha*, also formed the foundation of Joplin's own upbringing and beliefs.

Joplin was born on November 24, 1868, in Texarkana, Texas. His parents, Giles and Florence Joplin, stressed education as the key to success to their children, Monroe, Scott, Robert, William, Myrtle, and Ossie, just as Treemonisha's parents do.

Many of Joplin's compositions had a strong march beat and were played under a ragged, jazzy, rippling rhythm. This type of music was called ragtime. Joplin became known as "The King of the Ragtime Writers," and musicians came from miles around to try to outplay him, with little success. Joplin's instructions to "never play ragtime fast at any time" became his motto and appeared with the scores for most of his compositions.

Joplin believed that a ragtime opera could combine an established musical style with a new, more popular one. He composed three works that he hoped would bring ragtime the same recognition received by classical music: *The Ragtime Dance,* which was a ragtime folk ballet based on the dances of the time, and two operas, *The Guest of Honor* and *Treemonisha.*

After failing to find someone who would advance him the money to produce *Treemonisha,* Joplin decided to publish the 230-page score and present the opera himself. He barely managed to find enough singers and dancers to fill the parts, but the cast worked hard rehearsing the opera's twenty-seven musical numbers. Joplin did all the choreography for *Treemonisha.* He used dances from his childhood, such as the Reel, done by the cornhuskers, popular steps like the Cakewalk, and social dances of that time such as the Clean-up Dance, Jennie Cooks Dance, the Back-Step Prance, and the Stop Time. He also created a new dance, the Slow Drag, especially for the opera.

Treemonisha was first performed at the Lincoln Theater on 135th Street in Harlem in 1915. It was presented without costumes or scenery, before a small audience. Joplin couldn't afford to hire an orchestra, so he played the entire orchestral score himself on the piano. The production was not successful and received little, if any, attention from the press.

The failure of what Joplin considered his greatest work was almost too much for him to bear. He fell into a deep depression and suffered from strange mood swings—one moment extremely happy, the next without any energy at all. He also lost his ability to play the piano. Shortly thereafter, Joplin began destroying many of his unfinished works and musical sketches. He was afraid that people were stealing his music from him. His second wife, Lottie Stokes, finally had him committed to Manhattan State Hospital in 1916. He remained there, paralyzed and unable to recognize his friends, until his death on April 1, 1917, at the age of forty-eight. He was buried in St. Michael's Cemetery on Long Island, New York, on April 5, 1917.

Around the 1920s, a whole new generation embraced jazz. The popularity of ragtime began to wane, and, until the late sixties, the music had few fans. The decision to use Joplin's composition "The Entertainer" for the Oscar-winning movie *The Sting* in 1973 created a new audience for his work. Subsequently, many of his other compositions were rediscovered, recorded, and performed. *Treemonisha* was colorfully presented in a way Joplin could only dream it would be in Atlanta, Washington, D.C., Houston, and on Broadway in New York. The opera was a tremendous success and received a Pulitzer Prize in 1976.

Treemonisha is Joplin's tribute to the struggles of his past and his hopes for the future of his people. It is the crowning achievement of the work of a musical genius. Joplin once said that his music would not be fully appreciated until fifty years after his death. He knew that he was far ahead of his time. The continued popularity of his work proves that he was right.